The Boxcar Children Mysteries

THE BLACK PEARL MYSTERY

created by

GERTRUDE CHANDLER WARNER

Illustrated by Charles Tang

ALBERT WHITMAN & Company
Morton Grove, Illinois

ISBN 0-8075-0784-9

1 3 5 7 9 10 8 6 4 2

Printed in the U.S.A.

Contents

CHAPTER 1

Aloha Means "Hello"

"The captain has turned on the fasten seat belt sign to prepare for landing," a voice announced over the airplane loudspeaker. But six-year-old Benny Alden didn't hear a thing, for he was fast asleep.

Benny's older sister Jessie tugged her brother's seat belt to make sure it was buckled. Then she checked her young cousin's seat belt, too. "Wake up, sleepyheads," Jessie said to Benny and Soo Lee Alden, who were sitting on either side of her. "We're almost in Hawaii."

Benny opened his eyes halfway. "Are we there yet?"

Soo Lee pulled her blanket to her chin. "This plane ride is forever and ever."

Jessie patted Soo Lee's hand, then Benny's. "You've both been so good on this long plane ride. We've been flying for almost twelve hours." She pointed out the plane window. "Look down there."

Benny leaned over.

"Are all those islands part of Hawaii?" Benny asked when he looked out. "They look like a bunch of puzzle pieces on the ocean."

"The biggest ones are the seven Hawaiian Islands that people live on," Jessie explained. "One of them is Maui. That's the one we're going to. Soo Lee, do you remember when you stopped in Hawaii after Aunt Alice and Uncle Joe adopted you in Korea?"

The little girl yawned, then rubbed her big brown eyes. "The people put flower necklaces on us!" she said. "Now I remember."

Benny wriggled in his seat. "I don't want any old flower necklaces on me. But maybe one made out of sharks' teeth!"

Across the aisle, Grandfather, Henry, and Violet Alden laughed when they heard what Benny said.

"We'll soon find out about flower necklaces, sharks' teeth, and lots of other Hawaiian things," Grandfather said. "I just felt the landing gear go down. Just one more plane ride — a quick one, I promise — to Maui, then our Hawaiian vacation can really begin."

After so many hours on the big airplane, the half-hour flight to Maui felt like nothing to the Aldens. When they stepped off the small plane, the warm, clean air smelled of flowers.

A friendly woman greeted the Aldens as they entered the airport. "Welcome to Hawaii," the woman said. She was placing a flowered necklace called a *lei* over each passenger's head.

"I guess they ran out of sharks'-teeth

necklaces, Benny," Henry joked. "You'd better get used to wearing flowers. Look, everybody around here has on flowered shirts or pants or dresses."

Grandfather Alden searched the crowd. "That's going to make it hard to spot Joseph Kahuna. He manages my cousin Mary's pineapple plantation. She told me she'd send Joseph to pick us up and that he'd be wearing an orange flowered shirt."

"Hey! A man in a flowered shirt and a straw hat is holding up a sign with our name!" Benny said a few minutes after the Aldens collected their luggage.

Mr. Alden waved. "Good for you, Benny. I do believe that's Joseph Kahuna. It's been a few years since I've seen him on my visits to Hawaii. Let's go check."

Henry and Mr. Alden pushed two luggage carts toward the man, while the other children followed them.

"Joseph Kahuna," Grandfather said, shaking the man's hand, "James Alden here. Good to see you again."

The man checked a picture he was holding. Finally he spoke. "Aloha, old friend," he said. "Aloha, Alden children."

Benny tugged Mr. Alden's arm. "What does *aloha* mean?"

"*Aloha* means 'hello' *and* 'good-bye,'" Joseph Kahuna explained.

"We just said good-bye to our dog, Watch, and our housekeeper, Mrs. Mc-Gregor, back home in Greenfield. Now we're saying hello to everybody in Hawaii," Benny said. He decided to try out his first Hawaiian word right away. "Aloha, aloha," Benny said, greeting a woman who was trying to get Joseph's attention.

The woman ignored Benny. "Joseph!" she said in a loud voice. "I need a ride. None of the taxi drivers will go out to my estate. They say the old road is too muddy. I'd like you to drop me off."

Joseph Kahuna looked upset. "But — but . . . I have a full van of Mrs. Cook's guests. It's very crowded."

The woman, dressed in a black suit without a single flower, paid no attention. "I need a ride," she repeated in a louder voice.

"If Mrs. Cook ever expects to sell another pineapple to my canning factory, I'm sure she'd want you to drive me home."

Mr. Kahuna looked down at his work boots. "Of course, Mrs. Kane. I'll make room for you."

Mr. Alden tried to smooth things over. "Please join us. We're the Aldens. Any friend of Cousin Mary's is a friend of ours. We can put some of our luggage under the seats without any difficulty."

This didn't seem to make the woman any friendlier. "Well, I'm Norma Kane. Mary Cook and I are business acquaintances, not friends. I own a large pineapple plantation on Maui. I also just bought the canning factory on the other side of the island. If you're doing business with Mrs. Cook, then you'll be doing business with me as well. All the pineapple growers in this area sell their fruit to my cannery."

Mr. Alden nodded. "I see. While I'm in Hawaii, Cousin Mary and I will be discussing many different plans for her plantation."

"Hmph." Mrs. Kane then spread her briefcase and packages over the front seat without leaving room for anyone else.

The Aldens didn't really mind. They were just happy to be in Hawaii after their long trip. Mr. Alden and the children squeezed into the backseats of the van. They all settled down to take in the colorful scenery.

"Everything is so beautiful," ten-year-old Violet said. "I don't think I have enough colors in my paint box to match these trees and flowers."

Joseph Kahuna smiled in the rearview mirror. "Ah. I see the young lady loves our land. I'll be happy to give you a tour of our beautiful —"

"Joseph, can you go a little faster?" Mrs. Kane interrupted. "I must call my factory manager right away about the flooding. All the plantation owners are picking their pineapples before they rot in the fields. This means I can buy them at a very low price. Please speed it up so I can get home quickly."

Mr. Kahuna didn't answer right away. When he did, he spoke in a low voice. "I can only go at this speed, Mrs. Kane. The roads out this way are very poor, especially after all the rain. I, too, am needed as soon as possible."

"I wouldn't count on that, Joseph," Mrs. Kane said. "You may not have a job at Pineapple Place much longer. When I was in Honolulu, I heard that Mrs. Cook may be giving up her plantation."

Mr. Alden leaned forward from the backseat. "Oh, I wouldn't go that far. I know there have been problems with the pineapple crop. Still, this is valuable land. My cousin Mary would never give up her farm. I came here to help her figure out how best to run Pineapple Place."

"We came out here to help, too!" Benny piped up. "I can't wait to start picking pineapples."

Mr. Kahuna drove carefully over the twisty, bumpy road.

"Is the road always like this, Joseph?" Mr. Alden asked. "I can't believe you have to send your crops over a road like this one."

Before Joseph could answer, Mrs. Kane spoke up. "The state won't be fixing this old road. It doesn't pay. There's a new road under way from the other side of the island, where all the large farms are located. And it leads to my cannery. Soon all the pineapples on this island will come from large farms like mine — much more efficient."

Mr. Alden had a thing or two to say about this. "Well, that's one point of view. On the other hand, there's room for all sizes of farms in this state. Many tourists come here to see the sugarcane and pineapple plantations of old Hawaii, like my cousin Mary's farm. Not everyone in the world thinks bigger and faster are better."

With that, Mr. Alden rolled down the window to enjoy the breeze. The Alden children and Mr. Kahuna did the same.

After a long drive, the van stopped at a gate.

"Here's your estate, Mrs. Kane," Joseph announced. "Would you like me to drop you off here?"

Mrs. Kane gathered up her briefcase and packages. "Of course not! My house is at the end of this drive. I'll press the security button to open the gate."

After the gate opened, Joseph drove up the long, curved driveway. At the end stood a huge white house with a red tile roof.

"Let me help you with your bags," Joseph said when he pulled in front of the house. He collected Mrs. Kane's luggage, then followed her inside. When he returned about ten minutes later, Mrs. Kane was close behind him. She handed Joseph a piece of paper.

"You forgot this," she said. Joseph read what was on the paper and placed it on the dashboard of the van. He seemed awfully quiet.

"How many inches of rain have you had at Pineapple Place?" Mr. Alden asked.

Joseph drove on without answering.

"Were a lot of pineapples damaged?" Jessie asked, wondering why Joseph was so silent.

Finally he spoke. "I have to watch the road now. It's no good to talk."

The old road followed the coastline for about ten miles. Soon Joseph Kahuna's van passed sugarcane and pineapple fields, which lay like quilt squares on either side of the road.

Benny pointed to a cone-shaped mountain rising behind a sugarcane plantation. "Is that a volcano, Mr. Kahuna?"

Joseph drove without answering.

"Shhh," Jessie whispered to Benny. "Joseph needs to keep his eyes on this road. All the Hawaiian Islands were formed by volcanoes."

Soo Lee and Benny both opened their eyes wide.

"You mean we're riding on a volcano, Jessie?" Soo Lee asked.

"In a way," Jessie whispered. "I'll tell you more about it when we get to Pineapple Place. We need to be quiet so Joseph can drive."

Benny had a hard time being quiet. There was so much to talk about now that they were in Hawaii. He was glad when the van finally pulled into Pineapple Place.

The plantation was located high on a bluff that overlooked the ocean on one side and a mountain on the other. The farm was dotted with palm trees, nut trees, and trees with flowers the Aldens had never seen before. And, of course, there were fields of spiky pineapples in every direction.

Cousin Mary's house was small, but it had a large airy porch called a *lanai*. Benny spied a table of delicious-looking food. His stomach growled so loudly that he wondered if anyone else heard it.

Joseph led the Aldens out to one of the plantation's small cottages. It was freshly painted and inviting.

"This is so pretty," Violet said when the children stepped inside the three-bedroom cottage. The wicker furniture was painted white, and the beds were covered with flowered bedspreads. The children could hardly wait to take off their shoes. They wanted to feel the cool tile floor beneath their bare feet.

"Why did Joseph get so quiet after he dropped off that lady?" Benny asked Henry after Joseph left.

"I noticed the same thing," Henry said. "First he was friendly at the airport, then he wasn't. I don't know what Mrs. Kane told him, but he didn't seem friendly after he dropped her off."

Mr. Alden set down Soo Lee's suitcase. "Joseph has a lot on his mind. Perhaps Mrs. Kane reminded him of all the recent problems with Pineapple Place — the flooding, the poor roads. The small plantation owners out this way really need some help to keep going. That's why we're here."

"So that's why you're here!" the Aldens heard next.

Everyone turned around. A tall white-haired woman in overalls, work gloves, and rubber boots greeted Mr. Alden with a smile. "Aloha, Cousin James. Aloha, Alden children. I'm Cousin Mary. I'm delighted to meet all of you. I see Joseph has gotten you settled in the cottage. We just finished fixing it up. You're our first guests. Here's a pineapple right out of the field."

"Thank you, Mary. I know pineapples are a sign of welcome," Mr. Alden said. "This

young man is Henry. He's fourteen now. Next down is Jessie, who's twelve. Violet is ten. Then there's Benny, who is six. And our newest Alden is Soo Lee Alden, Joe and Alice's little girl."

Cousin Mary shook everyone's hands. "I'm so happy to meet all of you at last. I know all about how Cousin James found you living in a boxcar in the woods after your parents died and that he brought you home to Greenfield."

The children smiled, remembering the good old boxcar days when they had lived on their own. That was when they'd found their dog, Watch. Then Grandfather Alden had found them.

Mr. Alden put his arm around his cousin. "I didn't expect you to be looking so well after all the troubles you wrote to me about. Now that I've brought in my family, tell us how we can help."

Cousin Mary smiled again, though everyone could see she seemed tired. "You've already helped just by showing up with your grandchildren. People have been wonderful.

So many volunteers have arrived to help my workers harvest our pineapples quickly. Please don't worry, James. We've survived hurricanes, volcanoes, floods, insects, you name it."

"Sharks?" Benny asked. "Did you survive sharks?"

Cousin Mary laughed. "Before my husband died years ago, he saw sharks from time to time, but they never bothered him. Not to worry, though. You'll be swimming in our bays and coves, where the sharks don't go. Now, did Joseph tell you what's been going on here?"

Mr. Alden shook his head. "He was awfully quiet on the drive from the airport. We gave a woman named Norma Kane a ride home. He seemed to be upset after talking with her."

A shadow seemed to pass over Cousin Mary's face. "Ah, yes. Norma Kane. She just bought a large pineapple plantation and the cannery where we sell most of our pineapples. Old-time planters like me are all trying to get used to her new ways. But I'm sure we'll get along. Joseph was probably worried about the crop. We're picking pineapples as fast as we can before they rot in the wet ground. Many of my neighbors have come by to help out as well."

"We just have to unpack our suitcases so we can get into old clothes. Then we can pitch in, too," Jessie said.

Cousin Mary pushed back a strand of hair from her forehead. "Nonsense. You children need to relax — lie on our beautiful beaches, collect seashells."

"Ah, Mary," Mr. Alden began, "you don't know my grandchildren. You won't find them lying around on beaches. And they're not going to be collecting seashells when they can pick pineapples."

"And eat them, too!" Benny added. "Is that part of pineapple picking?"

"Eating pineapples is the best part of picking them," Cousin Mary said. "Now come out to the *lanai* for a bite to eat. It's time to start your vacation."

CHAPTER 2

The Legend of the Black Pearl

Mr. Alden left for Honolulu the next morning on business, and the children began their working vacation, too. First they tried on the rubber work boots Cousin Mary had given them.

"There's a pair for each of us, even small ones for Benny and Soo Lee." Henry held up two glove-covered hands and made a monster face. "I'm the volcano monster," he said. "Grrr."

The other children knew Henry was only fooling.

"You don't scare me with those big gloves, Henry," Soo Lee said. "Why do you have to wear them?"

Jessie read from a book opened on her lap. "It says here that pineapple plants have sharp leaves. The pickers have to wear the gloves so they won't cut their hands. Anyway, Cousin Mary said you and Benny and Violet don't have to pick pineapples. Instead you'll get to carry them to the carts after we pick them."

"Do I have to wear a straw hat?" Benny wanted to know.

Jessie nodded. "We all do so we don't get sunburned faces."

"Not me," Henry said. "I'm going to wear my baseball hat, only I left it in Joseph's van. Be right back."

"Would you bring back the travel books and brochures we picked up at the airport?" Jessie asked Henry. "I left them in the van."

Joseph Kahuna's van was still parked in front of the plantation house. Henry found his baseball hat on the floor. He quickly gathered up Jessie's travel books, papers, and brochures from under the front seat.

By this time, the other children were all set for pineapple picking. They came looking for Henry.

"I'll stick these papers and books in our cottage," Jessie said to Henry. "Cousin Mary said to meet Joseph out in the fields as soon as we were ready."

Sure enough, Joseph Kahuna waved the Aldens over the minute they appeared. Rows of pineapple plants stretched in every direction. The ground was muddy, with puddles everywhere.

"Over here, Aldens," Joseph said. "Since we can't send our machines into these muddy fields, we're picking pineapples the old Hawaiian way, with our hands. Then a runner carries them to these carts. Are there any good runners here?"

Benny's, Violet's, and Soo Lee's hands shot up. "We are! We are!" they cried.

The Aldens were glad to see Joseph smile again. "Very good. You three children will be my runners."

The children followed Joseph. He

stopped in front of a plant that was about the same height as Soo Lee. He took hold of the top of a pineapple. "These leaves on top are called the crown. You take hold of the crown and give it a twist." In a flash, Joseph was holding a large pineapple. "Now you try, Jessie."

Jessie reached down, grabbed the pineapple crown, and tugged several times. "Ta-da!" she cried when she finally pulled a pineapple free.

In no time, Jessie and Henry had picked several pineapples apiece. The younger children took turns carrying them down to the cart one by one.

By late afternoon, the carts were half full of ripe, juicy-looking pineapples. The Aldens were tired, but they kept right on picking along with the other workers and volunteers. Several people sang Hawaiian songs as they went along — sad songs and happy songs.

"Singing makes the work go faster, doesn't it, Jessie?" Violet said. "I wish I

knew what those words were. Maybe Joseph can tell us when we see him at dinner."

At five o'clock, the Aldens heard a loud bell ring.

"Day is done," a man named Luke from the next row over told the Aldens. "At six o'clock there will be a *luau*."

"I hope that means food," Benny said.

"A luau's a Hawaiian feast, Benny — roast pork, sweet potatoes, all kinds of Hawaiian fruits and vegetables," Luke said. "Some of the food is served on big banana leaves instead of plates. Mrs. Cook said she'd have a luau at the end of the day for the volunteers and workers."

Benny giggled.

"What's so funny, Benny?" Violet asked.

Benny couldn't stop giggling. When he finally did, he shared his joke. "I hope Cousin Mary Cook is a *good* cook!"

Everyone laughed. They hoped so, too.

At six o'clock, the Aldens joined the other pickers on the porch. After a hard day, everyone had showered and changed. Most of the men and boys wore colorful flowered shirts. The women and girls wore flowered dresses called *muumuus*.

A long table stretched along one side of the porch. The middle of the table was decorated with orchids and glass bowls of colorful, delicious-looking dishes the Aldens had never seen before. At the end of the table was a large square cake with coconut frosting.

"Don't be shy," Cousin Mary said, waving the Aldens in along with the other pineapple pickers. "A luau needs lots of hungry people. Now, please take a big banana leaf to use as a plate and help yourselves to the feast."

So the Aldens helped themselves. Spotting Luke and his five-year-old daughter, Hani, at a nearby table, the children came over with their food and sat down.

"Hi, Luke," Benny said. "I like eating from a plate that's made out of a leaf. I took lots of good things, but no pineapple. I had enough pineapple already!"

"Now have one of our famous fruit

drinks," Luke said. "It's made out of crushed fruit, coconut milk, and ice."

"Yum," Soo Lee said when she took a sip of a colorful drink Luke had poured from a glass pitcher.

The Aldens felt relaxed and happy. They were hungry and thirsty after a long day's work.

"I hope you've all left room for my special coconut cake," Cousin Mary said when she came around to the Aldens' table later. "But first we have to have some dancing and songs and stories. You can't have a luau without those."

"Or without coconut cake!" Benny added.

Everyone helped clear a space in the middle of the porch. First, a storyteller told tales about Hawaiian gods and goddesses and monsters who were said to live inside volcanoes. After the storyteller came several musicians. They played their steel guitars and *ukuleles*, which were like small guitars with just four strings.

Several dancers in real grass skirts came out and began to dance the Hawaiian dance called the *hula*. Though the Aldens didn't understand the Hawaiian words to the songs, they clapped and swayed when the music began.

"I know we don't have grass skirts, but can we dance, too?" Soo Lee asked Jessie.

Jessie turned to Luke when he got up to dance with Hani. "Do you think we should dance?" Jessie asked. "We don't know how to do the hula."

Luke smiled. "Just follow what Hani and I do. The movements in the hula dance tell a story or describe beautiful places on our islands. We'll get in front of you to show you the movements."

The Aldens were soon on their feet, waving their arms like Luke and Hani.

"That was fun," Violet said after the music ended. "What was the dance that we just did about?"

Luke leaned back and smiled. "It's about a secret waterfall where a god and goddess met and fell in love. We have many stories and legends in Hawaii. If I lived to be a hundred, I couldn't tell them all."

Hani pulled her father's ear. "Tell about the black pearl, Daddy, and all the bad luck. I want to hear that story."

Suddenly the Aldens noticed everyone at the table was quiet. People poked at their desserts with their forks or stared into their coffee cups. A few people looked at Luke.

"Please, Daddy," Hani begged. "Tell the story about the black pearl."

But Luke had no story to tell. "It's too late for that, much too late. Only Joseph Kahuna knows the real story of the black pearl, and I don't see him here tonight. It's time to go home, anyway."

Cousin Mary's luau was over. Everyone helped to clear the tables. No one spoke much.

"What was that all about?" Jessie asked Henry when the children went into the kitchen.

Henry shook his head. "I don't know, but everything stopped when Hani asked about the black pearl."

Cousin Mary turned around from the sink when she overheard this. "The black pearl?" she asked, her voice shaking. "Did Joseph tell you about it? I didn't even see him tonight, did you?"

The Aldens looked at each other. Why was Cousin Mary so upset?

"No, we saved some cake for Joseph, but we never saw him," Henry explained.

Soo Lee looked up at Cousin Mary. "Hani asked her daddy to tell the story about the black pearl. But he didn't want to. Can you tell us?"

Cousin Mary turned away. "The black pearl? I . . . really don't remember it. Maybe another time. Not tonight." With that, Cousin Mary put down her sponge, leaving the pots and pans in the sink.

"We'll finish up," Henry said. "Thanks for the good dinner."

One by one the children thanked Cousin Mary for the luau, too. But she stayed quiet. Soon she walked down the hall to her bedroom and closed the door behind her.

CHAPTER 3

A Mysterious Message

Waking up in Hawaii was like waking up in a jungle. Just outside the Aldens' guest cottage, several bright red honeycreepers twittered in the trees the next morning.

"Those birds are like little alarm clocks," Violet whispered to Jessie, who was half awake in the next bed.

Jessie yawned and looked over the side of her bed. "Where's Watch?"

The next thing Jessie felt wasn't Watch but Benny bouncing on the bed. "Watch isn't in Hawaii, silly," Benny said with a laugh. "But I am. Time for breakfast."

Jessie pulled the sheet up over her head. "You did a good job waking me up, just like Watch. I forgot we were in Hawaii, not Greenfield."

Benny tugged Jessie's covers. "Maybe our breakfast will be on banana leaves. Can I go now, Jessie? Cousin Mary said there's breakfast on the porch for the volunteers. That's what I am, right?"

Jessie opened one eye, then the other. She yawned. "You sure are, Benny. If you're really hungry, go ahead to breakfast now. We'll come in a while. Do you have your pink cup?"

Benny reached into his backpack. He took out the old cracked pink cup that he'd found when the children were all living in the boxcar. "It's right here."

So Benny went ahead. He just knew his first Hawaiian breakfast was going to be good. When he stepped onto Cousin Mary's porch, only one other person was there.

"Hi, Joseph," Benny said to Mr. Kahuna.

Joseph continued reading his newspaper without looking up.

This didn't stop Benny's chatter. "I'm an early bird, just like those honeycreeper birds with the funny beaks."

Joseph Kahuna turned the newspaper page.

"Is it okay to help myself?" Benny asked. He could hardly wait to try the juices, fruits, and breads spread out on the table.

"Go ahead," Joseph said at last. "The food is for everyone."

Benny poured some yellow juice into his pink cup, then took a sip. "Hey, this isn't orange juice!"

"It's papaya juice," Joseph said.

"Mmm, it's pretty good," Benny said. "What's this?"

"That's banana bread made from our macadamia nuts and bananas," Joseph said. "Everything on this table comes from this plantation. Those pineapples come from our plants, the papayas from our papaya trees, and the coconut milk from our palm trees."

"Did Cousin Mary's coconut cake last night come from a coconut cake tree?" Benny said with a twinkle in his eye. "We saved you a piece. Did you get it?"

Instead of laughing, Joseph just stirred his coffee. "I was called away last night. I missed the luau and the coconut cake."

Benny put down his cup. "It was fun. I liked eating, then dancing the hula and listening to scary Hawaiian stories." Benny took another sip of papaya juice before he continued. "And we almost found out about the black pearl. Luke and Cousin Mary said you know that story. Can you tell it?"

Joseph Kahuna put down his coffee cup so quickly, some of the hot liquid spilled over. He wiped it with a napkin. "The black pearl story is just an old made-up Hawaiian tale. Nothing to tell. Now I have to get to work."

"But . . . but . . . Cousin Mary said you knew about it," Benny said.

Joseph Kahuna stood up. "I know about pineapples. That's what I know about."

With that, Joseph Kahuna rose from his chair and left for the fields.

Benny loved to eat, but now he wasn't too hungry. He went back to the cottage.

When Benny arrived there, Jessie was reading aloud from a small piece of paper:

Please call me. I have something to discuss with you. No need to mention anything to Mary Cook or anyone else.
Norma Kane

"This was jumbled up with Jessie's travel books in the van," Henry explained to Benny. "We think something about this note upset Joseph after he dropped off Mrs. Kane."

"What do you think it means, Jessie?" Violet asked.

Jessie reread the note. "Do you suppose Joseph was at Mrs. Kane's last night? Why would he go there?" Jessie asked Henry.

"I don't know," Henry answered. "Let's just put the note back in the van. He might be upset that we saw it. I'll return it, then meet you at breakfast."

After Henry left, the other children

strolled to the main house for breakfast. Several volunteers and workers were seated on the porch when the Aldens met up with Henry and joined the buffet line.

"Over here," Luke said when he saw the Aldens. "We saved you some seats.

"Last day of picking," Luke told the children. "Then Mrs. Cook and a couple of our workers will drive the pineapples to the cannery. These pineapples are nearly ready now. We were lucky to save as many as we did. Too bad the pineapples in the back field aren't ripe yet. They'll be a loss because the plants' roots will rot in the muddy fields."

Henry put down his plate next to Luke. "Our grandfather had a good idea. He went back to Honolulu to help Cousin Mary get a loan. She'd like Pineapple Place to be a guest farm, too. That way she wouldn't have to depend only on pineapples."

"Cousin Mary wants to turn some of the workers' cottages into guest cottages like the one we're staying in," Jessie told Luke.

Luke took a sip of juice and thought about this. "Well, good luck to her. It's hard for visitors to get out this way. The roads are bad. Even the taxis and buses don't get out here much. And tourists don't always want to drive out so far in their rented cars."

Benny had an opinion about this. "My grandpa knows everybody, even Hawaiian people. I bet he can get the roads fixed."

Luke laughed. "You seem very sure of that, Benny. Fixing roads is a pretty big job. The government does that."

"Grandfather has an old friend in the state capital. That's where he is now," Jessie explained.

Luke smiled at the Aldens. "If anybody can do it, the Aldens can, I guess. You folks were picking pineapples yesterday like old hands."

Benny held up his hands. "But we have new hands! We're kids!"

Everyone around the table laughed.

Luke and Hani pushed back their chairs. "Well, time for picking. Coming along?"

The Aldens headed to the kitchen to drop off their plates.

"See you in a few minutes," Henry said

to Luke. "Maybe we can have a race to see who picks more pineapples."

Henry was wrong. When the Aldens arrived at the fields, there was no work for the children.

Joseph Kahuna avoided the Aldens. "I don't need you for picking today," he told them after they followed him into the fields. With that, Joseph walked to the back of a row of bushes, leaving the Aldens behind.

"What was that about?" Jessie asked.

Violet watched the other pickers working hard. "Didn't we do a good job?" she asked.

Jessie put her arm around Violet. "I think we did. Let's check with Cousin Mary."

The children found her in the parking area. She was supervising several workers who were loading pineapples into a pickup truck.

"Why, hello, Aldens!" she said. "What brings you here? I bet you needed a break. I've been feeling so guilty. You young people should not be picking pineapples in the hot sun."

Benny answered first. "But we weren't picking pineapples. Joseph wouldn't let us."

Now it was Mary Cook's turn to be puzzled. "Really? You know, Joseph isn't himself these days. Last night he missed the luau and didn't even tell me. I wonder what's going on. I wish he wouldn't worry so much about the plantation. Well, never mind. I have an even better idea."

"What's that?" Violet wanted to know.

Cousin Mary said, "We're dropping off most of our crop at the cannery. After that, there's a good time ahead. We'll set aside some of our pineapples to sell at the farmers' market in town. It's great fun. There are lots of food booths. I know you'll like that, right, Benny?"

"Food booths? I know I'll like that!" Benny answered.

Cousin Mary went on, "You can help me set up our booth, then you can take turns selling fresh pineapples to the tourists who visit the farmers' market. There are crafts, hula dancing, music, storytelling — all kinds of fun activities for children. You'll love it."

"We love it already," Jessie said. "As long as we're here, why don't we help you load this truck. The sooner we do, the sooner we can leave for the farmers' market."

So the Aldens set to work. They formed a line to pass the pineapples from the carts to the truck. They were very careful with the pineapples and held them as if they were babies. With five Aldens at work, the truck was soon filled.

"Done!" Cousin Mary said an hour later before she went into her house to change. "I'm glad Joseph didn't use you in the fields after all. This was a much better plan."

After Cousin Mary left, the children returned to their cottage to change from their work clothes, too.

"What I can't figure out is why Joseph didn't want us in the fields today," Jessie said. "He told us what a good job we did yesterday."

Benny pushed his straw hat back from his head. He was thinking. "Do you think I said something wrong?"

"What do you mean?" Jessie asked.

Benny swallowed hard. "At breakfast I asked him to tell me about the black pearl. He didn't like that. He turned away from me and everything. He wouldn't talk much. Was I being too snoopy?"

Jessie patted Benny's head. "Not to worry. You're just curious and not too snoopy. You can't help it."

"You know," Henry said, "this black pearl legend is a sore subject, that's for sure. Even Cousin Mary won't talk about it. Maybe Joseph didn't want us asking about the black pearl with Luke or any of the other workers around, so he kept us away from them."

"Or maybe he's just not himself these days, like Cousin Mary said," added Violet.

"I wish we could ask him," Jessie said.

But when Joseph Kahuna came by to drop off one more pineapple cart, he didn't give the Aldens a chance to ask him anything. He helped unload the last cart into the truck, then went back to the fields without even speaking to the children.

CHAPTER 4

Pineapples for Sale

After Joseph left, Cousin Mary slid behind the wheel of the plantation van. She called over to the Aldens, "Time to go. First stop is the cannery. Then on to the farmers' market in town. Hop in."

The Aldens crowded into the van. Cousin Mary followed the Pineapple Place fruit truck out of the plantation.

"My teeth are ch-ch-ch-chattering," Soo Lee said when the van hit one bump after another along the country road ahead.

"You can see the problems we're having,"

Cousin Mary said to Henry and Jessie, who were in the front seat. "It gets harder and harder to get my pineapples out and to get tourists to travel in this far."

"A bumpy old road doesn't stop us!" Benny cried.

Several empty trucks pulled away from the cannery parking lot when the Pineapple Place truck and Cousin Mary's van arrived. A worker with a clipboard waved the truck toward the warehouse in back. Cousin Mary followed the truck.

Then something strange happened. When the manager saw the van, he motioned it to stop.

"Why is he stopping us?" Jessie asked.

When Henry and Jessie took a second look, they noticed a familiar face. Norma Kane was in the loading area, too. She marched over to the van. "We're not taking any more pineapples, Mary. I bought the last load from the truck that just left here. You'll have to unload your pineapples elsewhere."

Cousin Mary took a deep breath before

she spoke. "I'm a bit confused, Norma. I understood from the previous owner that the cannery would buy the same number of pineapples as last year. In fact, I called your manager yesterday. He told me to have our truck arrive at ten o'clock. We even came a little earlier."

The cannery manager looked at Mrs. Kane. "It's true. I told her —"

Mrs. Kane broke in before the man could finish. "And I just told Mary no more pineapples today. We already brought in a truckload from my own farm, not to mention several truckloads from the large plantations down the road. How many pineapples do you think I can take, anyway? These small farms are hardly worth the bother."

Cousin Mary took another deep breath. "I had hoped you would buy the amount your manager agreed to over the phone. I know Pineapple Place is small, but our pineapples are very special. We counted on your word, Norma."

This didn't seem to bother Mrs. Kane a

bit. "My word is that I have quite enough pineapples for now."

Cousin Mary paused. "Someone's word and handshake used to be as good as money in the bank out this way. In the long run, that will turn out to be the best way to do business."

"I really don't have time to discuss these old-fashioned ways of doing things, Mary," Norma Kane said. "My manager will call you if we need your crop. No need to call us."

Cousin Mary looked as if she'd already put in a full day's work. "Well, I guess that's that. All we can do now is try to sell these at the farmers' market over the next couple of days. Everyone knows Pineapple Place pineapples are the best."

After Norma Kane closed the warehouse door, Cousin Mary's truck driver spoke up. "We can sell some of our crop at the farmers' market, Mrs. Cook, but a whole truck? That's not too likely. And these pineapples are nearly ripe, too."

The Aldens didn't know too much about

pineapples, but they weren't giving up so fast.

"We like to sell things," Jessie told Cousin Mary. "We've sold lots of things before. I know we can sell your pineapples. There are five of us."

"People like buying from kids," Benny added. "We sold lemonade in Greenfield. We made lots of money. Almost five whole dollars!"

For the first time that day, Cousin Mary smiled. "You know, I have a feeling if anyone can sell pineapples, it'll be you Aldens. Let's get going."

The Aldens wasted no time setting up a colorful booth at the farmers' market in the middle of town. Violet quickly made up some posters. Jessie and Henry learned how to use the juice machine. Soo Lee and Benny poured fresh pineapple juice into small cups. They handed out free cups of juice to the many tourists and shoppers who passed by.

"Fresh, juicy pineapple juice here!"

Benny said when people went by. "Fresh, juicy pineapples, too!"

At first the Pineapple Place booth was a big success. But, awhile later, the crowd seemed to disappear.

"Where did everybody go?" Benny wanted to know.

Mary Cook soon had an answer. "Norma Kane's workers set up a booth down the block," she told the Aldens. "They're selling pineapples at half the price I have to charge. If I lower my prices, I might as well dump my pineapples into the ocean."

"Oh, no," Jessie said. "Is there anything we can do?"

Cousin Mary took off her straw hat. "I wish. But I had my driver make several calls to canneries on the other side of Maui — even on some of the other islands. It's the same story everywhere. All the rain forced growers to pick their crops at the same time and sell to the places they used in the past. There are too many ripe pineapples and not enough canneries. No one is interested in a whole truckload of pineapples."

By midafternoon, most of the shoppers and tourists had gone home or back to their hotels.

Cousin Mary folded up the bright blue market umbrella. "You children did an amazing job. I've never sold so many pineapples at the farmers' market in one day."

The Aldens tried to feel happy about this, but how could they? Cousin Mary's truck looked almost as full as it had been that morning.

"It's okay, children," Cousin Mary said when she saw how discouraged the children looked. "Be proud of yourselves. You couldn't have unloaded more pineapples if you'd given them away for free. I make most of my money selling my crop to the cannery. Still, this farmers' market money will help, too. Now I want to share some of the profits with you. Here's five dollars each. Go buy yourselves some souvenirs while I close up the booth."

Henry pushed the money away.

Even Benny wouldn't take anything.

"When we go places, we like free souvenirs the best — like rocks and treasures we find."

Cousin Mary hugged Benny. "You children are the best treasures I could ever find. Well, at least go buy some ice cream. Try coconut ice cream if you want a real treat. You can window-shop while I pack up everything. You've worked hard enough."

Ten minutes later, the children stood in front of a jewelry store and enjoyed their ice-cream cones.

"Wow!" Benny said, when he saw all the diamonds, pearls, and gold in the window. "Do all those jewels come from Hawaii?"

"Some of them do," Jessie answered. "The pearls anyway. I remember reading about that in my geography class. People used to dive for pearls in the oyster beds in Hawaii. There's even a bay called Pearl Harbor off Oahu, only it's not used for pearl farming anymore."

"Do farmers grow pearls like pineapples?" Soo Lee asked.

Jessie smiled. "Not exactly. A pearl grows

inside an oyster shell when something small like a grain of sand gets stuck in it. There's a pearly liquid inside the oyster that covers the grain layer by layer. After a few years, you get a pearl! On pearl farms they put some kind of tiny bead or grain in the oysters on purpose."

Violet pointed to a gold chain with three grayish pearls in the middle. "I wonder where they found those dark ones. The sign says they're black pearls. Can we go inside and find out why they're dark like that? Maybe the owner knows something about the legend of the black pearl."

The children finished up the last of their ice-cream cones, then entered the shop.

Inside, the owner was talking with two customers who were facing away from the Aldens. He sounded impatient. "I can't tell you the value of something that disappeared over forty years ago. Even my own father never saw it, and he was an expert in pearls."

One of the customers spoke softly, but

the Aldens could still hear what she said: "Just give us an idea, that's all. We'd like to know what it's worth."

Before the owner could answer, the bell over the shop door jingled. A group of tourists crowded into the shop.

"Sorry," the owner said. "I have to wait on these customers. Anyway, I really don't have the information you want. People around here think it's bad luck to even talk about it. Good day."

The Aldens overheard the couple arguing on their way out.

"I told you not to say anything," the man said. "No use stirring things up by asking a lot of questions. Now come on, let's find a place to stay."

Violet strolled over to the counter. "Can you tell us about the black pearl —"

Before Violet could finish, the owner tapped his pencil on the glass counter. "Again? I really haven't time to discuss these old stories while I'm so busy."

Violet stepped back. "Sorry. I just wanted

to find out about the black pearl necklace in the window. I wondered why the pearls are dark, not white."

The owner calmed down a bit when he heard this. "Oh, sorry, young lady. I thought you were asking about something else. Black pearls come from the black oysters. They only grow in a couple of special bays around the Hawaiian Islands. They're pretty rare, even small ones like that. The big ones — well, I've only heard about them. Does that answer your question?"

Violet nodded. "Yes, thank you."

"The store owner told us about the necklace," Henry said to the other children after they left the jewelry store. "But he wouldn't talk about the black pearl legend. I'd sure like to know what's so mysterious, anyway. Nobody around here wants to talk about it."

The children dawdled along, stopping at a booth where someone was making leis with blossoms, feathers, even nutshells. At another booth, a woman was weaving a hula skirt from long plant leaves.

"I'd like to wear one of those grass skirts," Soo Lee said. "Maybe Hani will let me try one of hers."

The Pineapple Place booth was closed when the children turned the corner about a half hour later.

"Look who Cousin Mary is talking to," Violet said. "I didn't get a close look, but those two people seem like the couple we overheard in the jewelry store."

Cousin Mary waved to the children. "Come meet Richard and Emma Pierce. They stopped to ask for directions, and what do you know? They're looking to buy a small farm out our way. They need a place to stay while they look at farms for sale. They can stay in my other guest cottage for a while."

Benny looked at the couple. "Hi! Were you just in the jewelry store down the block?"

Mr. and Mrs. Pierce didn't answer right away.

Finally Emma Pierce spoke up. "We've been walking around looking at all these booths. It's too nice out to be shopping indoors."

"But . . . but . . . you sound just like the people we heard talking about —" Benny stopped. His brother and sisters had taught him good manners. "Maybe it was two other people," he said finally in a soft voice.

"All the shops and booths are crowded," Richard Pierce told Benny. "It's easy to get mixed up."

But Benny wasn't mixed up at all. He had sharp ears. He was sure that the people in the jewelry store were the same couple standing in front of him. Why didn't they just say so?

CHAPTER 5

Voices in the Night

Even without pineapples, Pineapple Place was busy. There were nuts to gather, papayas to pick, and chores to do all around the plantation.

Over the next couple of days, Cousin Mary couldn't get the Aldens to relax. "I have wonderful workers to take care of the jobs around here," she told the children as they helped clean up after another delicious dinner one night. "I won't let you lift another finger without doing some of the things you came to Hawaii to do, starting with snorkeling. That's your job for tomorrow morning."

"Snorkeling isn't a job," Benny said. "It's just fun. We learned how in Florida."

Cousin Mary was pleased to hear this. "Good. Then I know you'll have a good time snorkeling in Hawaii. We have underwater lava formations and caves not far from here. Cousin James said you brought your own equipment. My husband drew some maps of his favorite snorkeling places. They're in my office on my desk, so just —"

A crash of silverware on the tile floor interrupted Cousin Mary.

Emma Pierce stood in the doorway, with a knife, fork, and spoon at her feet. "Sorry," she said, bending over to pick up the dropped silverware. She quickly put her silverware on the counter, then left the kitchen as quietly as she had entered.

"The Pierces are a funny pair," Mary Cook told the Aldens. "They seem never to be around, then they suddenly appear when I don't expect them. Now I want you children to disappear for a walk on the beach. The moon is totally full tonight. You won't even need a flashlight. You'll see lots of little sand crabs and sea creatures on the beach. Go have a good time."

As always, the Aldens did as they were told. The children climbed down the wooden steps that led from the plantation to Pineapple Bay. Cousin Mary was right. In the moonlight, the children could see sand crabs darting in and out of the gentle waves.

"Know what?" Benny said. "Those two people always seem to be around, just like Cousin Mary said."

"I know what you mean," Jessie joined in. "This morning after we ate breakfast with Cousin Mary on the porch, I ran back to get my hat. Emma Pierce was standing off to the side of the porch. She walked away fast when she saw me. I had a feeling she'd been listening in."

"For people who said they wanted to go look at other farms," Henry said, "they seem to hang around Pineapple Place a lot."

The children soon forgot about the

Pierces. There was a completely full moon shining over the bay. Everything was silvery in the moonlight.

"I wish I could paint a picture of this," Violet whispered.

The children were quiet, enjoying the sound of gentle waves lapping on the beach.

Soo Lee, holding Violet's hand, stopped. "I hear music. And a person's voice."

The children listened.

"I hear a ukulele," Jessie said. "Somebody's saying something, too. Maybe some of the workers came down to the beach."

The children followed the sound of the voice and the ukulele. Soon they came to a steep, rocky point that separated Pineapple Bay from Reef Bay.

"Can we climb up?" Benny asked.

"Cousin Mary said people do it all the time," Henry said. "Here, I'll go up first and give you a hand if you need help."

The children scrambled over the rocks until they came to the bluff overlooking Reef Bay. In the distance, a campfire flickered on the beach. There seemed to be a man and several children sitting by the fire.

Jessie put her finger to her lips. "Shhh. I think it's Joseph and his grandchildren. Let's listen."

"Grandfather, tell us the black pearl story again," the Aldens heard a child say when they got closer. "We like that best of all."

In the firelight, the Aldens saw Joseph pick up his ukulele. He strummed a few notes, then began to tell a story.

Over five hundred moons ago, on a faraway island in Hawaii, there lived a poor young diver. He had the same name as you children have now — Kahuna — which means "one who knows secrets." Young Kahuna knew all the secrets of the sea: where the best fishing could be found, where the dangerous tides would be, where the finest oysters lived at the bottom of the ocean.

Young Kahuna dived for pearls nearly every day of his life. No one could dive deeper or stay underwater as long. He discovered more pearls than any diver had ever found.

The Kahuna family was soon able to buy

land. There they grew the juiciest pineapples and fruits on the island. Nearby they built a large, sun-washed house, close to the ocean that had been so good to them. For their son, they built a fine sturdy boat to sail across the sea.

One day young Kahuna dived deeper than he had ever dived before. At the bottom of the sea, he touched the largest oyster he had ever felt. He dropped the heavy oyster into his diving net. With his lungs nearly bursting, he swam to the surface and gasped for air. He could hardly wait to open his treasure.

With his sharp diving knife, he finally opened his oyster. There, resting inside, was the largest pearl he had ever seen — a rare black pearl! In his excitement, he stepped on a poisonous fish sleeping on the sandy bottom of the bay. His foot felt as if it were on fire. Still, he could only think of his pearl and the new riches it would bring to his family.

When he reached his family's house, he could barely walk from the pain in his foot. Yet, he held on to his pearl. He showed it to his mother and father. "We are rich!" they cried, proud of their son.

But woe, young Kahuna fainted from the pain in his foot. For many days, then many months, the poison infected his whole body. He could no longer dive, no longer fish, no longer swim like a dolphin in the sea.

Then more terrible things happened. His father's boat crashed upon the rocks, and his father was never seen again. Thieves broke into the house looking for the famous black pearl. One such thief knocked over a lantern and set the beautiful beach house ablaze. Insects arrived in a cloud one morning and ate all the pineapple blossoms on the bushes. There were no pineapples that year.

Young Kahuna, still sick from his infected foot, began to fear for his mother and for his own life. The black pearl was cursed. This he knew. So he visited an old Hawaiian fisherman who knew about such things. The man told young Kahuna that his bad luck would not turn to good luck again for five hundred moons. To avoid more bad luck, the pearl must be given away or returned to the sea.

Young Kahuna offered the pearl to a mainlander who had come to Hawaii to seek his fortune. But alas, the black pearl brought the new owner bad luck as well. So the man hid the black pearl in an underwater cave where it would curse him no more. In five hundred moons, when the bad luck turned to good, the man planned to dig up the pearl again.

Here, Joseph Kahuna stopped talking and simply played his ukulele. But his grandchildren asked for more.

"Where is the black pearl now, Grandfather?" the Aldens heard a little boy ask.

"It is said that the pearl remains hidden in an underwater cave. All these many moons, no one has searched for the pearl for fear of its dangerous powers." Then Joseph began to sing a Hawaiian song that the Aldens did not understand.

"What a story!" Jessie whispered before she and the other children turned away.

They walked along the ridge until they reached the rocky point again. As the children climbed up, they heard rocks tumbling down the other side.

"What's that?" Benny asked. "Is somebody else out here, too?"

"Slow down," Jessie reminded everyone. "These rocks are tricky, especially at night."

The five Aldens climbed carefully to the top of the point. They stared down at the Pineapple Bay beach ahead of them.

"Is that a person running over there?" Benny said, pointing ahead.

"Yes," said Jessie. "But it's too dark to tell who it is."

At that moment, a large cloud passed over the moon. By the time the moon was clear again, the beach looked empty in the moonlight.

The sky grew cloudy. The children felt tired. Jessie and Henry held out their hands to help the younger children climb down the rocks. By the time they reached the Pineapple Bay beach, only the sand crabs were out and about.

Cousin Mary was sitting on the porch, listening to the radio when the Aldens came in.

Benny and Soo Lee ran over to her rocking chair.

"It was so pretty outside," Soo Lee said.

"There were lots of sand crabs," Benny told Cousin Mary. "And shiny jellyfish, too. But we didn't step on any."

Even in the dim light, the children noticed how worried Cousin Mary looked.

"We just came to say good night. Thank you for telling us to take a walk. It was a beautiful night out," Violet said.

Cousin Mary didn't seem to hear Violet at first. Finally she looked up at the children. "Did you . . . did you happen to see Norma Kane at all when you were out? She came by looking for Joseph, of all people. I told her to check the old beach shack where he sometimes spends his nights off. I'm terribly worried Norma is trying to hire him away from Pineapple Place."

The Aldens looked at one another. They didn't know quite what to say.

"No, we didn't see Mrs. Kane," Jessie said honestly. "We hardly saw anyone out tonight."

CHAPTER 6

Shark Warning!

That night, Jessie had trouble sleeping. She awoke several times. Finally she decided to get some fresh air. She stepped onto the back porch of the guest cottage. The moon was high in the sky, casting its silvery light over Pineapple Bay.

Jessie walked over to the telescope Cousin Mary had left on the porch for the children. She turned the telescope this way and that, trying to find stars, but the moonlight made most of them too faint to see.

"A shooting star!" Jessie said when she spotted a light moving across Pineapple Bay. "Oh, it's just a boat," she whispered to herself. "It's stopping."

Jessie couldn't see much else. She was tired again, so she went back inside and climbed into her warm, cozy bed.

Slip-slap. Slip-slap.

"What's that sound?" Jessie called out as she packed a duffel bag with snorkels, masks, and fins the next morning. When she turned around, she started to laugh. "Oh, it's you, Benny, in your snorkeling fins! You sounded funny coming into the room."

Benny stood in the doorway of Jessie's bedroom. A snorkeling mask covered his eyes, nose, and mouth. On his feet were big yellow swimming fins.

"I'm ready," he said after he took off his snorkel and mask.

"I'm ready, too," Jessie said. "Henry asked us to meet him in Cousin Mary's office. We're going to pick up those underwater maps she told us about. Are Soo Lee and Violet ready?"

They were ready. The Aldens had learned all about snorkeling on a trip to Florida with Grandfather Alden. They knew how to breathe through a snorkel. They knew how to keep their masks from getting fogged. Best of all, they knew how much fun snorkeling could be. They couldn't wait!

"I'm glad I ran into you. Just go right in my office for those maps," Cousin Mary said. "I'm heading into town on errands this morning. I had Joseph set out bag lunches for you and the Pierces on the porch. I told the Pierces I'd be out all morning and that all of you should just help yourselves."

Something was still bothering Henry about the night before. "Did Joseph say anything about last night? I mean about seeing Norma Kane or anything?"

A shadow seemed to pass over Cousin Mary's face. "He told me he didn't see her. I'm still concerned that she'll hire him away from Pineapple Place. I gave him the next few days off when he asked me. Maybe he needs some time to think. Oh, dear. Here I am gabbing on and on about my troubles. Now off you go to my office for those maps. I left them right on top of my desk for you yesterday afternoon."

The children headed for Cousin Mary's office. First they checked her desk, but the maps were nowhere to be seen.

"Let's check underneath the desk and behind the furniture in case the maps slipped off," Henry suggested.

The Aldens got on their hands and knees behind the desk. That's when they heard the office door squeak open. They all popped up at the same time.

Richard Pierce stepped back from the doorway, startled by the sight of the five Aldens. "What are you kids doing here?"

"Cousin Mary told us we could pick up something she left for us that we need for snorkeling," Jessie said simply.

Emma Pierce, standing behind her husband, quickly stuffed something into her tote bag. "Let's . . . uh . . . go, Richard. Obviously Mrs. Cook isn't here. We just . . .

mmm . . . wanted to ask her about some farms for sale down the road. See you later."

Richard Pierce had one last thing to say to the Aldens. "If you're going snorkeling, I'd stay away from Reef Bay. There are reports of shark sightings."

After the Pierces left, Henry seemed puzzled. "It's pretty strange. Cousin Mary said she told the Pierces she would be going to town this morning. Why did they come to her office when they knew she was gone?"

Jessie shook her head. "There's something about those two I can't figure out. As for the maps, I guess we'll just have to ask Cousin Mary about them when she gets back. And we'd better forget about snorkeling out at Reef Bay. We don't want to meet up with any sharks."

On their way to Pineapple Bay, the children passed the Pierces' rented car. Jessie noticed their trunk was open. "Should we shut it for them, Henry?"

"Know what?" Henry said. "I'll run to their cottage and ask them. Maybe they were just unloading their — hey, look what's in there. Scuba-diving equipment, tanks, hoses, and all kinds of deep-diving gear. I didn't know the Pierces were —"

"Now what are you kids snooping around here for?" Richard Pierce demanded. "You didn't touch anything, did you?" He slammed the trunk shut.

Jessie swallowed hard. "Henry was just about to look for you to tell you the trunk was open. We would never bother other people's things."

Richard Pierce looked upset with himself for yelling at the Aldens. "Sorry. The equipment belongs to someone else. I didn't want anything to happen to it, that's all."

Henry felt better. "I know how to scuba dive, too. When my grandfather comes back, he's meeting a marine biologist friend who dives around here. She's going to lend me some scuba equipment so we can explore some of the local reefs and caves. Would you like to come along when we go?"

"This equipment belongs to someone else," Richard Pierce repeated before he turned around and walked away.

"Why doesn't he want to go scuba diving, Henry?" Benny asked after Mr. Pierce left. "If I knew how, I would go diving with you and Grandfather's friend."

"Mr. Pierce didn't really answer that question, Benny," Henry answered. "Hey, with all the excitement, we forgot something."

"Our lunch!" Benny cried. "My stomach didn't forget that."

The Aldens returned to the main house. Joseph was arranging the lunch bags Cousin Mary had left behind for the guests.

"Hi, Joseph," Violet said in a quiet voice. "We came to pick up our lunches before we go snorkeling."

Joseph nodded. "Here they are. Mrs. Cook had me fill one thermos with coffee for the Pierces. The other one is juice for you children. I put a juice cup in each bag with the sandwiches. Good day."

"We hope it's a good day," Jessie said. "But we just heard there might be sharks in Reef Bay."

Joseph Kahuna wasn't so quiet with the

children now. "Who said such a thing? Sharks don't swim in our bays. Why, a shark is a creature that needs the whole ocean for its home, not a small bay. In all my many years of living on the bay, I haven't seen or heard of a shark in Reef Bay or any other bay nearby, not even an injured shark. Someone is making up a story."

"We like stories but not that one," Benny told Joseph. "Before we go back to Greenfield, can you tell us the black pearl story like you told your —" Benny stopped when he felt Henry tap his hand. "Sorry, never mind."

"You are like my grandchildren, always wanting another story. I have many stories. As for the black pearl, there is nothing much to tell. It was a rare jewel that brought bad luck to everyone. Its last owner . . ." Joseph stopped talking for a minute. "Yes, the last owner of the pearl threw it into the sea, and that's where the story ends. Now I must be going. I'll be away for a few days on another part of the island. Good-bye."

The children packed their lunches into their beach bags. They headed for the steps that led down to the beach. They were nearly there when Henry spoke up.

"You realize, don't you, that Joseph told us a different story than the one he told his grandchildren?" Henry asked the other children.

Jessie took off her sandals and walked along the water's edge. "Yes, he just said the last owner of the black pearl threw it into the sea, but he told his grandchildren the pearl was hidden in a cave. And he didn't mention anything about the five hundred moons passing. That's about forty-two years ago. I wonder if Joseph was the young man in his story. He seems about sixty now, so he could have been eighteen then."

"Maybe Joseph *is* searching for the black pearl," Henry said.

"I wonder if other people are searching for it, too," Jessie said.

CHAPTER 7

Underwater Mystery

With Jessie leading the way, the children hiked along the Pineapple Bay beach.

"This is a good snorkeling spot," Jessie said. "Pineapple Bay is peaceful, and there are no sharks! My guidebook says there are some lava formations near the shore. So what are we waiting for? Let's get our equipment on."

Henry and Jessie helped the younger children slip into their life jackets. They helped one another adjust their goggles so the water wouldn't leak in. Finally they all walked backward into the water wearing their fins, just like experienced snorkelers.

The Aldens snorkeled along the shore in shallow water. This made it easy for the younger children to stand up if they grew tired. The children waved at one another underwater and pointed to a school of parrot fish that swam right by. Jessie took Soo Lee by the hand, and Henry took Benny's hand. They pointed down to underwater sea fans swaying in the gentle current. Several tiny angelfish fed on other plants.

The Aldens floated along, enjoying the underwater world of colorful fish and rocks.

After a while, the children stood up.

"I saw lots of minnows!" Soo Lee said. "I tried to touch them, but they swam away."

"Let's take a little break right now," Jessie suggested. "When you're snorkeling, it's easy to forget the time. We don't want to tire ourselves out or lose track of where we are."

Violet pushed her mask up on her forehead. "I'll stay on the beach with Soo Lee

and Benny if you and Henry want to snorkel some more."

Jessie smiled. "Thank you, Violet. Henry and I took that special snorkeling class in Florida. I'd like to go farther on, out by the reefs near the rocky point. I just wish we had those special maps Cousin Mary told us about. We'll be back in about twenty minutes, okay?"

The younger children settled on the deserted beach and began to build a sand castle. Jessie and Henry snorkeled farther out to the coral reefs. After a while, Henry waved Jessie over. He pointed to something up ahead. Jessie caught up with Henry. She and her brother were in deep water now. They were strong swimmers and good snorkelers. They knew how to stay afloat without getting too tired.

"I think I just spotted some kind of underwater cave down there, Jessie," Henry said while treading water. "At least that's what I think it is. The tide is coming in, and the water's getting rough, so it's hard to see what's down there. Want to take a look?"

Jessie bit down on the mouthpiece of her snorkel and swam by Henry's side. An underwater cave! That would be something to see.

Henry swam above the cave, which looked to be five or six feet below the surface. "I'm going to dive down, Jessie. Here, hold my snorkel."

Like an arrow, Henry dived down toward the cave entrance. But the current kept him from getting too close, no matter how hard he swam. He thought he saw a metal object inside, but he ran out of breath and came to the surface.

"I saw something shiny, like metal, inside that cave, but I couldn't check it out no matter how hard I tried," he told Jessie. "I'm afraid we're caught in a strong current."

"I thought so," Jessie replied. "I guess that's why the snorkeling seemed so easy at first. The current carried us all the way out here to Reef Bay. We'd better get out of it right now before we tire ourselves out and get in trouble."

Henry and Jessie swam across the current as they had been taught. Their plan worked. After a few minutes, they were close to the shore again. They were so glad when they felt solid ground beneath their feet.

"Whew," Henry said. "Too bad I couldn't get down to that cave. I'd like to find out what that silvery object was. I guess I'll have to scuba dive down there if I get a chance."

Jessie took several deep breaths in a row. "I'd like to find out what that was, too. Hey," Jessie said, waving to a figure up on the nearby hillside. "Somebody's watching us. Can you tell who it is?"

Henry squinted, but the person stepped away. "Whoever it was is gone. Well, never mind. Let's head back to Pineapple Bay."

Jessie and Henry walked along the shore for nearly fifteen minutes until they reached the rocky point that separated Reef Bay and Pineapple Bay.

"I guess it would be safer to climb the rocks the way we did last night," Henry said.

"Oh, I think I see Benny up ahead,"

Jessie said when she and Henry stood at the top of the rocky point. "At least, I see a speck moving around the beach."

Sure enough, the speck on the beach turned out to be Benny. He was running up and down the beach and skimming flat stones over the water. Nearby, Violet and Soo Lee were putting the finishing touches on their sand castle.

"There you are!" Benny cried when Henry and Jessie joined him. "Did you see any sharks?"

Henry chased Benny and lifted him into the air. "No. Did you?"

Benny laughed. "Not on the beach, silly!"

Jessie put away the snorkeling gear in her duffel bag and pulled out a pair of binoculars. "Let's go back up to those rocks. I want to take another look over Reef Bay to see if we can figure out where the cave is. Let's leave our snorkeling gear here in this bag. There's not a soul on the beach to worry about."

The children walked a bit until they

reached the rocky point. It was much easier climbing to the top during the day than it had been the night before.

"Here." Henry handed the binoculars to Benny when the children reached the top of the ledge.

"There's a boat out there where you're pointing, Henry," Benny said.

Henry bent down to help Benny focus the binoculars.

Benny held the binoculars steady. "Now I see the boat better. It's a little red sailboat, only the sails are down. Someone is swimming near the boat, but I can't tell who it is."

Jessie checked her watch. "We should be getting back. Grandfather's going to call us this afternoon from Honolulu. I don't want to miss his call."

The Aldens climbed down from the rocks. They walked along the shore until they spotted the sand castle the younger three children had built.

"Where's our snorkel bag?" Violet asked.

"You put it down right by our sand castle, didn't you, Jessie? I hope the ocean didn't wash it away."

Jessie shook her head. "The water is calm here. Besides, the sand castle would have been washed away, too, and it's not even wet."

The children walked back to the palm trees behind the beach. There was no snorkel bag to be seen.

Jessie was upset. "I should've been more careful. I thought it was fine to leave our bag here since no one was around."

Soo Lee, being the littlest Alden, noticed something the other children had missed. She pointed down at the sand. "Someone was on the beach. Look at the footprints. We don't have such big feet."

Sure enough, a set of footprints led away from the sand castle into the rain forest behind the beach. Whoever made them had worn shoes or sandals with V-shaped markings — someone with much bigger feet than any of the Aldens.

CHAPTER 8

Sleeping Volcano

That afternoon, Cousin Mary returned to Pineapple Place just as the Aldens returned from snorkeling. "Such long faces! Is anything the matter?" she asked when she noticed how quiet the children were. "Was the water too cloudy for snorkeling? Sometimes that happens if it's windy."

At first the children didn't answer.

Finally Jessie spoke up. "Our snorkeling equipment disappeared from the beach after we went snorkeling. We don't know what happened to it."

Benny could hardly stand still. "Somebody with big feet came to the beach. We saw footprints and everything!"

This surprised Cousin Mary. "Goodness! We never lock a thing around here. This part of the island is so safe. Perhaps the tide carried it off. Why, I once lost a picnic basket that way."

"But the waves didn't wash our sand castle away," Soo Lee told Cousin Mary. "And know what? There were feet marks. They were bigger than Henry's feet, even!"

"I see," Cousin Mary said. "Well, I'll have to look into this. But not to worry, you can go snorkeling again. I always keep snorkeling equipment available for my guests, even my young guests. Now tell me, before your snorkels disappeared, did you find any of those coral reefs my husband marked on his maps?"

"That's another thing," Jessie answered. "We checked your office for the maps you told us about, but we couldn't find them."

Cousin Mary looked puzzled. "How

strange. I left the maps right on top of my desk for you. I hope no one else borrowed them. They're the only ones I have. Oh, dear."

Jessie and Henry looked at each other.

"Actually, the Pierces came to your office, but they didn't seem to know about the maps when we told them what we were doing there."

"Know what? They said we couldn't snorkel in Reef Bay. Know why? 'Cause of sharks!" Benny suddenly remembered.

"Sharks in Reef Bay?" Cousin Mary cried. "Nonsense. Reef Bay is far too small for sharks to swim in. They don't know much about the ocean, that's for sure. They probably thought you should snorkel in a shallow area. Well, I'll just have to search for those maps myself. But first let me tell you about a wonderful outing I've planned."

The Aldens couldn't wait to hear.

"How would you like to visit a volcano early tomorrow morning?" Cousin Mary asked.

Benny immediately forgot the missing snorkels and fins. "Will the volcano be hot and bubbly?" he asked.

Cousin Mary grinned. "Not this one. Haleakala Crater is a sleeping volcano. It hasn't been active for over a hundred years, but the crater it left behind is quite a sight."

Soo Lee looked up at Cousin Mary with a serious face. "The volcano won't wake up when we go there, will it?"

Cousin Mary put her arm around the little girl. "No, it won't, Soo Lee. Scientists can tell ahead of time if a volcano is going to act up. But Haleakala is still taking a nice long nap."

"Shucks," Benny said. "I'll run away fast if it starts boiling up!"

"That won't happen," Cousin Mary told Benny. "You'll get to see something very special instead — the sun rising up over the crater. It was formed after the volcano blew up a long time ago. Haleakala is the largest crater in the whole world."

Watching the sunrise wasn't nearly as exciting to Benny as watching a volcano blow up, but he didn't say so. Going to the top of the biggest crater would be fun, too.

"We need to arrive at the crater rim by sunrise. That means leaving here about three o'clock in the morning," Cousin Mary explained. "You'll have to go to bed very early."

Soo Lee rubbed her eyes. "That's okay. The beach made me tired."

The thought of going to bed made the other children yawn and rub their eyes, too. They'd had a long day.

"Jessie and I had to fight a current to get back to shore," Henry said. "We won't have much trouble falling asleep early tonight. Don't worry, though. We'll be up in time for the sunrise."

Very early the next morning, Mary Cook's van arrived at the top of the Haleakala Crater. The children had slept for most of the two-hour trip up the long, winding road. They awakened when Cousin Mary turned off the engine. There was a stiff breeze when everyone got out of the van at the visitors' center.

"Good thing you brought your fleecy jackets to Hawaii," Cousin Mary told the Aldens. "The temperature at the crater rim is much colder than down below. We're ten thousand feet above sea level."

The children stretched out and yawned. At five o'clock in the morning, the sky was still dark. They walked to the rim of the crater but couldn't see much in the darkness.

Benny took a quarter from his pocket. "When it gets light, can I look through those telescope things and see if I can find our cottage?"

Cousin Mary laughed. "These telescopes aren't sharp enough to see that far, Benny. Still, you can see for miles from up here. The crater is nearly seven miles long."

Jessie rubbed her eyes. "That reminds me of something. The other night I couldn't sleep very well, so I got up and looked through the telescope on our porch. I thought I saw a boat heading for Reef Bay. It looked as if it left from the Pineapple Place dock. Then it stopped moving."

"Are you certain of that, Jessie?" Cousin Mary asked. "I can't imagine anyone going out that late. Joseph has his sailboat at his beach shack in Reef Bay. As for my boat, it's available for my staff and for guests, but no one has asked me about taking it out."

Jessie yawned. "Now I'm not sure what I saw. I was just so tired from waking up over and over. Maybe I dreamed it!"

Cousin Mary waved the children over to the lookout. "Well, you're not dreaming this. See that tiny ray of light way across the crater? That's the sun's first light. One Hawaiian legend says that a magician named Maui caught the sun with a rope to slow it down over the crater so his mother's laundry would dry. That's why the sun seems to take so long rising over Haleakala."

Henry looked around at the other small groups of shivering tourists. Many of them aimed their cameras at the other side of the crater where the sun was rising. The Aldens didn't take out their camera right away. They wanted to watch the amazing sunrise with their very own eyes.

"Wow!" Benny said, along with other visitors when a huge orange ball lit up the sky. Ever so slowly, it rose over the biggest hole Benny had ever seen in his life. The sun looked almost as big as the earth itself, climbing in slow motion over the crater.

"You can see why *Haleakala* means 'House of the Sun,'" Cousin Mary told the Aldens.

For the next hour, Cousin Mary and the Aldens sat on the crater rim and enjoyed the bright morning sunshine. The cold air had made them hungry. They enjoyed the delicious egg sandwiches and hot cocoa Cousin Mary had brought along.

After breakfast they stopped by the gift shop in the visitors' center. The children wanted to send postcards to Alice and Joe Alden and to Mrs. McGregor.

"Can I write something to Watch?" Benny asked Violet.

"Sure, Benny," Violet said. "Go ahead."

Benny drew a smiley face for Watch, then printed his name.

"You children can sleep all the way back

to Pineapple Place," Cousin Mary said when they climbed into the van to go home.

"I'm not sleepy," Soo Lee said.

"Me neither," said Benny. But within minutes after the van had started, the five Aldens fell fast asleep. They didn't wake up again until Cousin Mary stopped for gas not far from Norma Kane's cannery.

Henry climbed down from the van to pump the gas for Cousin Mary. The other children stretched and yawned, happy to be awake after their long naps.

"Look, a pineapple truck from the Kane plantation is in front of us," Henry told Cousin Mary after she drove away from the gas station.

Cousin Mary noticed the truck, too.

Violet could see Cousin Mary's puzzled face in the rearview mirror. "I thought they didn't need any more pineapples at the cannery."

Cousin Mary slowed down the van. "I'm going to pull to the side of the road here and run into the cannery. It can't hurt to ask Norma whether she can use more pineapples after all. Ours are still good for juice."

The pineapple truck from the Kane plantation pulled off the road in front of the cannery, too. Before Cousin Mary even turned off the engine, the truck driver got out.

"Goodness! It's Joseph!" Cousin Mary cried. "Why is he driving Norma Kane's truck? He told me he needed a few days off. He never mentioned anything about working for Norma." She took a deep breath and leaned her head against the steering wheel.

"This is so awful," Violet whispered from the backseat. "Why would Joseph do that?"

Cousin Mary restarted the van. "I don't know. I just don't know."

CHAPTER 9

Wiki Wiki

When Cousin Mary and the Aldens returned to Pineapple Place late that afternoon, they had a surprise.

"Grandfather!" Jessie said when she spotted Mr. Alden strolling by Cousin Mary's house. "You're back early. We've been pineapple picking and snorkeling and visiting an old volcano and all kinds of things."

Cousin Mary looked especially pleased to see her cousin James Alden. She needed to put Joseph Kahuna out of her mind for a little while. "I'm so glad you returned

96

early, James. What a nice surprise."

"Now I'm the one to be surprised," Mr. Alden said. "Didn't you get the message that I would be arriving today?"

Cousin Mary looked confused. "What message?"

"Why, last night I left a message with a woman who answered the phone," Mr. Alden said. "I told her I would be returning this morning, and that I'd be meeting Dr. Charlotte Lilo here. You remember I mentioned Charlotte? She's a marine biologist at the university. You didn't get the message?"

Cousin Mary shook her head. "No, I'm afraid I didn't. I wish I knew who took it, because maybe I missed other phone messages as well."

Mr. Alden looked upset. "This is a shame, it truly is. You see, Charlotte is just stopping over on Maui until tomorrow morning. She was looking forward to going snorkeling with the children this afternoon. And she even planned to bring Henry scuba diving. Now it's so late in the day, I'm not sure —"

At that moment, a tanned, middle-aged

woman strolled up to the group. "Hello, Aldens! I'm Dr. Charlotte Lilo."

"Are you a fish doctor?" Soo Lee asked.

Dr. Lilo laughed. "In a way. I'm studying the fish and reefs around the Hawaiian Islands to find out how to keep them strong and healthy."

Mr. Alden introduced Charlotte to the children and to Cousin Mary. "Sorry they came back too late to go out on the water with you, Charlotte. No one received the message about my return."

Dr. Lilo didn't seem to be a bit bothered by this. "No problem, James. We'll just go snorkeling and diving at night. In many ways, you can see a lot more underwater at night than during the day. We'll go out as soon as the sun goes down."

"Night snorkeling— neat," Benny said.

Even Cousin Mary looked pleased at the new plans. "You'll take my boat. One of my workers, Luke, knows many good snorkeling spots around here. Luke!" Cousin Mary called out when she saw him approaching. "We were just talking about you."

"I found the snorkels you keep for guests, Mrs. Cook," Luke said. "They're clean and ready for the Aldens."

"Luke, I'd like you to meet Dr. Charlotte Lilo. She's going to go night snorkeling and scuba diving with the children. I was wondering if you would mind bringing everyone out to the reefs in my boat tonight."

Luke put out his hand. "Glad to meet you, Dr. Lilo. I've heard all about your work in saving our coral reefs. I'd be glad to take you and the Aldens out diving and snorkeling. How about meeting me at the dock at eight o'clock tonight?" he asked everyone.

"See you then!" Dr. Lilo answered.

Just before eight o'clock that night, the Aldens decided to stop by Cousin Mary's office to let her know they were leaving. Jessie knocked on the office door, which was half open. "Cousin Mary! Are you in there?"

"Oh, come in, children," Cousin Mary answered. "I found my husband's maps. I was just checking some snorkeling spots he had marked. Show them to Luke and Dr. Lilo before you go out in the boat."

Henry and Jessie came around the desk. They looked over Mary Cook's shoulder and read the hand-drawn maps.

"These are the maps?" Jessie asked. "Where were they?"

Cousin Mary put down the maps. "Why, right here, on top of the desk where I left them," she told the children. "Are you sure you didn't put them with your things by mistake? They're wet from salt water."

The children gathered around. Sure enough, the maps were still damp.

"These maps weren't on the desk at all when we were here yesterday," Jessie said. "We looked all over. Maybe someone else borrowed them to go snorkeling." Jessie remembered the Pierces, but she didn't say anything. After all, anyone on the plantation might have borrowed the maps as well.

Cousin Mary put on her reading glasses again. "No harm done, in any case. Now take a look at this spot over here that's

marked with an X. The maps are so out of date, these caves are completely underwater now. In the old days, they were in fairly shallow water at low tide. But hurricanes and currents have changed the beach since then. Now the only way to reach the caves is to swim out to them as you did yesterday or go out by boat. *Wiki wiki*, children."

"*Wiki wiki?*" Soo Lee asked.

"*Wiki wiki* means 'Hurry, hurry'!" Cousin Mary said, shooing the children toward the door.

Cousin Mary's motorboat was already running when the Aldens met Dr. Lilo and Luke at the dock.

Luke set down a large metal can. "We're all set. I checked the gas tank for leaks, and there's no problem. It's funny. I filled the tank the other day, but I had to refill it just now. I wonder if one of the other workers or guests took the boat out. Anyway, we're fine now. I have life jackets for everyone. Dr. Lilo stowed the scuba and snorkeling gear in the hatch. So step in."

Dr. Lilo and the Aldens found seats in the boat. Then they set out toward Reef Bay, where the best snorkeling spots were.

A few minutes later, everyone spotted a larger boat stopped in the water up ahead.

"That's one of the cargo boats," Luke said, slowing down. "Some of the plantations ship their fruit across Reef Bay by boat. I wonder why it's out at night and why it's anchored here. Usually cargo boats head straight to the cannery or warehouse docks to unload their fruit."

"It's marked Kane Plantation," Henry said, looking through the binoculars.

Luke slowed down. "Can you take over the controls, Dr. Lilo? I'd like to check out that boat. Why would it anchor all the way over here? Maybe it's in trouble."

As Dr. Lilo steered the motorboat closer, the cargo boat pulled away quickly.

Luke tracked the boat with the binoculars, but it was too dark to see much. "It's the Kane boat, all right. I could've sworn they just pulled up a scuba diver. Pretty strange for a cargo boat to be used for scuba diving," Luke said.

Luke slowed the boat, then cut the motor. "Here's where we drop anchor. The underwater caves are close by."

Dr. Lilo and the Aldens double-checked their snorkeling and scuba equipment and life jackets. They were ready.

"You can jump in, dive in, or just step down from the boat," Luke said.

Luke and the younger children stayed in the boat. After Dr. Lilo did a last-minute check of Henry's scuba tanks, she, Henry, and Jessie slipped into the water.

Dr. Lilo, Henry, and Jessie each had underwater spotlights. They were amazed at the underwater world, which was so alive with fish even at night.

Jessie pulled out her disposable underwater camera. She took a picture of Henry entering a cave. She had just clicked a picture when she heard a loud horn on the surface. She lifted her head. A large boat was moving in their direction.

"Sharks around here," someone on the boat shouted to Luke and the children. "You should get everyone out of the water real quick."

Jessie didn't waste a second. She dived down to warn Henry and Dr. Lilo.

A few minutes later, Henry, Jessie, and Dr. Lilo surfaced, then swam back to the boat and climbed in.

"What a shame we had to cut our dive short," Dr. Lilo said. "I've never heard of sharks swimming in the bay. That would be very unusual behavior for a shark. I'll have to check into this."

Henry was even more disappointed. "I'd really like to return here another time. I'm pretty sure that was the cave I saw when you and I went snorkeling, Jessie. This time I got inside."

"Did you see the silvery object you spotted yesterday?" Jessie asked.

Henry shook his head. "I didn't see anything. It looked just like the same cave, but whatever I saw inside yesterday has disappeared."

CHAPTER 10

Aloha *Means "Good-bye"*

When the Aldens arrived at breakfast the next morning, Cousin Mary and Grandfather Alden were discussing future plans for Pineapple Place.

"Well, Mary, I'm sorry I couldn't arrange that bank loan on this trip. I know how disappointing that is," Mr. Alden said. "But I found out that the senator will get going on those road repair funds that have been tied up for the last couple of years."

Cousin Mary stared into her coffee cup. "Yes, thank you, James. Having good roads out this way will be a big help in a couple of years. Of course, I'd hoped for the bank loan for a few things. Now that Norma Kane won't buy our crop, some of the small owners are renting space on a charter plane to ship our pineapples to Korea in two days. The loan would have made that possible. It would also have given me some money to fix up two or three more cottages so I could rent them out to tourists."

Grandfather Alden patted Cousin Mary's hand. "I know we're leaving tomorrow, Mary, but I've made some excellent contacts in Honolulu. I'll follow up with phone calls to the banks, don't you worry."

Cousin Mary tried to smile. "All of you have been so helpful. I wish you'd come at a better time when everything wasn't upside down."

"Like pineapple upside-down cake?" Soo Lee asked. "I ate that for dessert last night."

Now Cousin Mary smiled a real smile. "Yes, like pineapple upside-down cake, Soo Lee."

"Now tell me about the visitors who

rented the other guest cottage," Mr. Alden said. "How are they enjoying their stay? Maybe they'll spread the good word to their friends about a Pineapple Place vacation."

Cousin Mary didn't speak right away. Instead she reached into one of the folders in front of her. She handed Mr. Alden a piece of paper. "Read this, James."

Mr. Alden read the note aloud:

Dear Mrs. Cook,
Thanks for renting us the guest cottage.
Sorry we didn't stay the whole two weeks.
Here's a check for five nights.
                    Richard and Emma Pierce

"I'd been hoping the Pierces would stay the whole time," Cousin Mary began, "since money has been so tight. I think I upset them last evening when I asked if they had borrowed my husband's old maps. The next thing I knew, they left. Very odd people."

"How so?" Mr. Alden wanted to know.

Before Cousin Mary could answer, Benny

spoke up. "They wouldn't go scuba diving with Henry even though they had tanks and fins and everything. And they didn't know anything about sharks. And then they tried to snoop in the office, but we scared them away!"

Mr. Alden couldn't help laughing. "Did you, now? Well, I guess it's time to go back to Greenfield if you're scaring away Cousin Mary's paying guests."

"Nonsense," Cousin Mary said, laughing along with Mr. Alden. "Your grandchildren are the best advertisement for Pineapple Place. In fact, I made copies of a flier Violet drew to tell tourists about the plantation. I only have the two guest cottages fixed up right now, but it's a start. We're going to hand the fliers out at our farmers' market booth this morning."

And that's just what the Aldens did later that morning. Not a tourist went by the Pineapple Place booth without one of the Aldens handing out a flier. Several people spoke to Cousin Mary about renting a guest cottage on future trips to Hawaii. Things were looking up.

Of course, no one went by the booth without Benny and Soo Lee handing out free pineapple juice. Their farmers' market business was a success.

"You children have put in enough time here," Cousin Mary told the Aldens at lunchtime. "Your grandfather and I can cover the booth ourselves. It's your last day. I want you to take a lunch break and do some sightseeing."

"Goody," Benny said. "I'm going to have barbecued sweet potato chips and papaya juice. And that's just to start."

So the Aldens went off in search of lunch at the many nearby food stands. They strolled along the rows of tables offering everything from fresh oysters to grilled shark. Mostly, though, the Aldens tried things that looked a little like food they ate at home.

"Sweet potato chips are like Mrs. McGregor's homemade potato chips when we have hamburgers," Benny announced. "Except they're sweet!"

When the children finished eating, they decided to go window-shopping one last time.

"Let's see if anybody bought the black pearl necklace," Violet suggested.

The Aldens rounded the corner where the jewelry shop was. They saw someone they knew rushing down the street.

"Joseph!" Henry called. "Wait up!"

The children ran ahead, trying to catch up with Joseph Kahuna. But Joseph didn't hear the Aldens. He dodged in between people as if he were being followed.

He *was* being followed.

Just a few feet behind him, Norma Kane made her way through crowds of people, never getting closer to Joseph.

"Joseph!" Henry called again.

This time Joseph stopped and stared at the Aldens. He looked upset.

"What's the matter with Joseph?" Soo Lee asked. "He's running away."

Indeed he was. He crossed the busy street, not looking back.

"Joseph just dropped something in the middle of the road!" Benny cried. "Some kind of box, I think."

Joseph turned around and stepped off the curb into the street again to pick up the box. A truck was coming, though, so he had to wait.

Finally the WALK light flashed on, and the Aldens were able to cross the street. Henry quickly scooped up the metal box. He led the children safely to the other side, where Joseph was standing.

Henry handed Joseph the box. "Here, this is yours."

"Thank you. You saved something very, very important. Look." Joseph pried off the box lid and opened a smaller container. Inside was a glowing black pearl — perfectly round and larger than any pearl the Aldens had ever seen. Joseph let the younger children hold the pearl.

"Oooh," Soo Lee and Benny said, their

eyes wide with amazement as they each held the pearl in turn.

At that moment the traffic stopped, and Norma Kane suddenly appeared in front of them.

"That's mine!" she said to Benny. "Hand it over. It came from waters near property I own."

Benny's fist tightened around the pearl. He looked up at his brother. "What should I do, Henry?"

"Hand it over!" Norma Kane repeated.

Henry took a deep breath. "Let's go find Cousin Mary and Grandfather. They'll know what to do."

When the Aldens and Joseph arrived at the booth, Richard and Emma Pierce were talking with Cousin Mary.

"Joseph!" Cousin Mary cried. "What are you doing here?" Then she noticed Norma Kane. "Oh, dear, I suppose you're going to quit and work for Norma. I knew that was coming when I saw you driving her truck the other day."

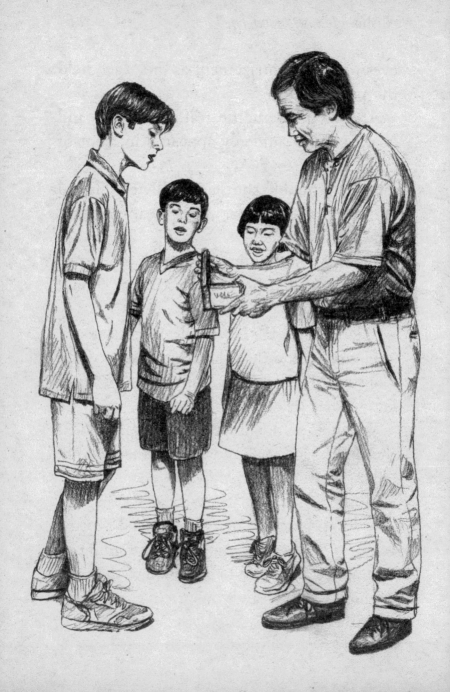

Joseph looked upset. "I wouldn't leave Pineapple Place, Mrs. Cook. I only worked a couple of days for Mrs. Kane after she told me she might buy your pineapples if I helped out with her harvest. When I drove her home from the airport, she gave me a note to meet her the night of the luau to make the arrangements. That's all."

"Hmmph!" Norma Kane said. "There is no way I would hire someone who stole something that belongs to my company. Open your hand, little boy," Norma Kane ordered Benny.

Benny unclenched his fingers one by one. The black pearl rested in the middle of his hand, which he clenched up again.

"Oh, the black pearl!" Cousin Mary whispered. "Where did you find it? And *how* did you find it?"

Joseph sat down to tell his story.

"The Aldens really found it, Mrs. Cook," Joseph began. "One afternoon, I was walking along the bluff over Reef Bay to get to my shack. I saw Henry and Jessie snorkeling out past the rocky point. A while after that, I heard them talking about something silvery Henry saw in a cave. You know, Mrs. Cook, when the wind is right, even whispered words can travel clearly over the water. After Henry and Jessie left the beach, I took my sailboat to the spot and dived down until I found the cave and this box inside the cave. I was just taking it to a jewelry store to find out its value."

Norma Kane stood there, steaming mad. "The Kane Plantation borders the waters where those caves are, so they're part of my property as well."

This was too much for Mr. Alden. "I'm afraid the law wouldn't agree with you. Property rights do not extend into the ocean, Mrs. Kane. In any case, may I ask how you learned about the location of the cave?"

Mrs. Kane didn't answer, but Jessie did.

"You overheard Joseph tell the legend of the black pearl the night the moon was full, didn't you?" Jessie asked. "Cousin Mary said you were going to look for Joseph that night. We overheard the story, too."

"And we heard rocks falling down and, know what? We saw someone on the beach, but we couldn't tell who it was," Benny said.

Mrs. Kane looked away. "It's no use. You might as well know. I was on the beach. I hired a scuba diver twice to go out in my cargo boat to look for the black pearl. I told the pilot to chase anyone away by saying there were sharks."

Now the Aldens looked confused.

"Sharks? The Pierces said that, too," Henry remembered. He turned to the Pierces. "Did you know about the cave and the black pearl, too?"

Richard Pierce shook his head. In a quiet voice he answered Henry's question. "We took Mr. Cook's old maps to go look for the cave. We're treasure hunters, but it looks as if Joseph got there first."

"Are you scuba people, too?" Benny wanted to know.

"We're scuba people, too," Richard Pierce confessed. "We borrowed the Pine-apple Place boat a couple of times, once at night, and tried to find the caves, but the bay has changed since your husband drew those maps."

Cousin Mary looked upset now. "So you took my husband's old maps without asking?"

Emma Pierce nodded. "I'm so sorry. I was about to return them, but the children were in your office when we tried to put them back. I returned there later on. That's when Mr. Alden called to say he was coming back early, but I forgot to give you the message."

Cousin Mary reached into her pocket and handed Emma Pierce a piece of paper. "Please take back your check. I don't want any dealings with you and your husband."

Richard Pierce walked over to his car. When he returned, he handed Jessie her duffel bag. "I took more than the maps, young lady. I'm really sorry. Here's your snorkeling bag. Emma and I got carried away with the idea of this black pearl. We didn't want some kids upsetting our plans to find it."

"Look, we're really sorry," Emma Pierce said to the Aldens and Cousin Mary. "I see now that the black pearl brought us bad luck. It made us do things — bad things — that we wouldn't normally do."

Jessie took the duffel bag without a word.

Soo Lee looked down at the ground. "You do have big feet," she said to Richard Pierce. "Bigger than Henry's, even."

This made nearly everyone smile a little before the Pierces got in their car and drove away.

Benny was still clutching the black pearl in his hand.

"May I?" Cousin Mary asked Benny. Though her hands were shaking, she held up the pearl. "So this is the pearl that brought my husband so much bad luck? If only Hiram had thrown it into the ocean as the old fisherman told Joseph to do. Instead, Hiram wanted to keep it and hide it away. Everything went wrong after that," she whispered.

Mr. Alden put his arm around Cousin Mary. "There, there," he said. "It's only a story. Hiram wasn't the only one in Hawaii who ran into bad luck. Hawaii is beautiful, but starting a new life here isn't always easy, Mary."

Cousin Mary handed the pearl to Joseph. "Here, Joseph. Now that the five hundred moons have passed, maybe it will bring you good luck. You found the pearl. It's rightfully yours."

"I suppose you won't be needing that job, then, will you?" Norma Kane asked Joseph. "It's too bad, because after I reached my goal of buying up the rest of the small plantations, I would have made you the manager of all of them."

Joseph Kahuna took the pearl in his hand. "No, rich or poor, I was never going to take your job. You see, I grew up on a small plantation, then I worked for Mr. and Mrs. Cook's plantation. Working hard is what changed my bad luck to good luck, not the moon or this pearl. Anyway, the pearl is rightfully yours, Mrs. Cook. I gave it to your husband. Please take it back. You can fix up Pineapple Place like a palace now. You can even send our harvest off on that plane in two days. This pearl is worth a great deal of money."

Cousin Mary looked happier than the Aldens had ever seen her. "Friends like you, Joseph, and a family like Cousin James and these dear children — they're worth more than money."

Everybody was smiling and hugging, except for Norma Kane, of course. And Benny.

"Is this worth more than money?" Benny asked when he dug something out of his pocket.

"What's that?" Joseph asked when Benny held up a tiny gray pebble.

"It's a black pearl, I think. I found it on the beach. Is it worth anything?"

"It's worth our whole trip to Hawaii!" Grandfather Alden said, laughing.

GERTRUDE CHANDLER WARNER discovered when she was teaching that many readers who like an exciting story could find no books that were both easy and fun to read. She decided to try to meet this need, and her first book, *The Boxcar Children*, quickly proved she had succeeded.

Miss Warner drew on her own experiences to write the mystery. As a child she spent hours watching trains go by on the tracks opposite her family home. She often dreamed about what it would be like to set up housekeeping in a caboose or freight car — the situation the Alden children find themselves in.

When Miss Warner received requests for more adventures involving Henry, Jessie, Violet, and Benny Alden, she began additional stories. In each, she chose a special setting and introduced unusual or eccentric characters who liked the unpredictable.

While the mystery element is central to each of Miss Warner's books, she never thought of them as strictly juvenile mysteries. She liked to stress the Aldens' independence and resourcefulness and their solid New England devotion to using up and making do. The Aldens go about most of their adventures with as little adult supervision as possible — something else that delights young readers.

Miss Warner lived in Putnam, Connecticut, until her death in 1979. During her lifetime, she received hundreds of letters from girls and boys telling her how much they liked her books.